A NOTE TO PARENTS

When your children are ready to "step into reading," giving them the right books—and lots of them—is as crucial as giving them the right food to eat. **Step into Reading Books** present exciting stories and information reinforced with lively, colorful illustrations that make learning to read fun, satisfying, and worthwhile. They are priced so that acquiring an entire library of them is affordable. And they are beginning readers with an important difference—they're written on four levels.

Step 1 Books, with their very large type and extremely simple vocabulary, have been created for the very youngest readers. **Step 2 Books** are both longer and slightly more difficult. **Step 3 Books,** written to mid-second-grade reading levels, are for the child who has acquired even greater reading skills. **Step 4 Books** offer exciting nonfiction for the increasingly proficient reader.

Children develop at different ages. **Step into Reading Books,** with their four levels of reading, are designed to help children become good—and interested—readers *faster*. The grade levels assigned to the four steps—preschool through grade 1 for Step 1, grades 1 through 3 for Step 2, grades 2 and 3 for Step 3, and grades 2 through 4 for Step 4—are intended only as guides. Some children move through all four steps very rapidly; others climb the steps over a period of several years. These books will help your child "step into reading" in style!

For Karen
—B.B.

For Sidney
—C.S.

Library of Congress Cataloging-in-Publication Data:
Brenner, Barbara. / Beef stew / by Barbara Brenner ; illustrated by Catherine Siracusa.   p.   cm.–(Step into reading. A Step 1 book) / SUMMARY: When his friends decline to come over for a beef stew dinner, Nicky feels bad until a surprise visitor shows up.   ISBN: 0-394-85046-7 (pbk.); 0-394-95046-1 (lib. bdg.)
[1. Dinners and dining–Fiction] I. Siracusa, Catherine, ill. II. Title. III. Series: Step into reading.
Step 1 book.   PZ7.B7518Be   1990   [E]–dc20   89-36769

Manufactured in the United States of America   13   14   15   16   17   18   19   20

STEP INTO READING is a trademark of Random House, Inc.

Step into Reading

Beef Stew

By Barbara Brenner

Illustrated by Catherine Siracusa

A Step 1 Book

Random House New York

When Nicky woke up,
he smelled something good.
What was that good smell?

It was beef stew!

"I am making lots of stew,"
said his mother.
"Would you like to ask
a friend for supper?"

"Yes!" Nicky shouted.
He ran off to school
to find a friend—
a friend who liked beef stew.

At school Nicky saw Alec.
Alec was his best friend.
"Can you come for supper?"
asked Nicky.

"Sorry," said Alec.

"I have to go to the dentist."

At lunch Nicky went to sit
with Carla.
"Can you come for supper?
It's beef stew."

Carla shook her head.

"I like hot dogs.

I like burgers.

I like pizza.

But I do not like beef stew!"

Later Nicky went
to the library.
Mr. Blake found
just the right book for him.

So Nicky asked Mr. Blake
to come for supper.
Mr. Blake was sorry,
but he could not come.
"My family is going
to eat out tonight."

On the way home
Nicky looked for a friend
to come for supper.

But he did not find anyone—
anyone who liked beef stew.

Nicky turned the corner.

There was a friend!

"Hi, Officer Gabel,"

Nicky shouted.

"Can you come for supper?"
asked Nicky.

"It's beef stew."
But Officer Gabel
could not come.

"It's my birthday.
There's a party
at the station tonight."

"Happy birthday,"
said Nicky.
He headed down the street.

Nicky saw the garbage man.

But the garbage man

never said hello.

He was not a friend.

And Nicky did not ask him

for supper.

Now Nicky was almost home.

And he felt sad.

He kicked a pebble

down the street.

"No one wants to come
for supper tonight.
No one wants to eat beef stew,"
Nicky said to himself.

"Boy! Do you look sad,"
someone said.
Nicky looked up.
It was Mr. Cone.
"Maybe this will cheer you up."

Mr. Cone handed Nicky

a post card.

Nicky read the post card.
He started jumping
up and down.
"Hooray!"

"Bye, Mr. Cone!"
Nicky called.

Nicky ran all through town,
past the police station,
past the garbage truck,
past his school.

Nicky ran all the way
to the train station.
A train was pulling in.
People got off.

Nicky saw her right away.
He rushed up to her.

His grandma hugged him.
"What a surprise!"
she said.
"I see
you got my post card."

And that is how
Nicky brought a friend home
for supper.
A friend who liked beef stew!